This book belongs to

_____

Based on the TV series *Nick Jr. The Backyardigans*™ as seen on Nick Jr.®

SIMON SPOTLIGHT
An imprint of Simon & Schuster Children's Publishing Division
1230 Avenue of the Americas, New York, New York 10020

The Backyardigans
Ready-to-Read
Treasury

Ready-to-Read

SIMON SPOTLIGHT / NICK JR.
New York   London   Toronto   Sydney

Contents

Surf That Wave!
page 9

Castaways!
page 33

Riding the Range
page 57

Rescue Patrol
page 81

Trouble on the Train
page 105

A Royal Valentine
page 129

Three Wishes
page 153

Super Spies
page 177

Surf That Wave!

adapted by Christine Ricci
based on the teleplay by Janice Burgess and McPaul Smith
illustrated by Susan Hall

Hi! I am Pablo.

I am a surfer.

This is my surfboard.

I see a wave.

I paddle my surfboard.

I ride the wave!

Watch this!

I can jump!

I can spin!

I can do a flip!

Oops!

Wipeout!

I do it all over again!
I love surfing!

adapted by Alison Inches
based on a script written by Leslie Valdes
illustrated by Warner McGee

"Ahoy, there!" says .

UNIQUA

"Ahoy! We are castaways!"

say  and .

PABLO   TYRONE

35

"Our  was lost at
SHIP
sea!" says 🐧 .
PABLO
"Our ⬭ had a leak!"
LIFEBOAT
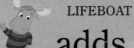 adds.
TYRONE

"Now we are stuck on an ," says .

ISLAND   PABLO

"We are the only ones here," says .

TYRONE

"I am a castaway too,"

says  .

AUSTIN

"I feel very shy today."

"I feel too shy
to say 'ahoy' to ,

UNIQUA

, and 🦬."

PABLO   TYRONE

"We need to build a HUT

in case it !"

RAINS

says .

PABLO

"I will look for

WOOD

for the walls."

"Wow," says  .

PABLO

"Where did all of this

wood come from?

Ahoy! Is somebody there?"

41

"I will look for
VINES

to tie the ,"
WOOD

says .
TYRONE

Snip! Snip!

"Hey," calls .
TYRONE

"Who cut these ?
VINES

Ahoy! Is somebody there?"

"I will look for
LEAVES
for the roof," says .
UNIQUA
Swish! Swoosh!

 fall to the ground.

LEAVES

"Ahoy! Is somebody up in

the 🌴 ?" asks 🐛 .

TREE   UNIQUA

The castaways bring the

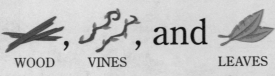, , and 🍃

WOOD   VINES   LEAVES

back to the 🏖️.

BEACH

They build their .

HUT

"Wow! We built a nice

 ," says .

BEACH HUT UNIQUA

"Now all we need is food to eat," says .

TYRONE

"Maybe we can catch a ," says .

FISH   UNIQUA

"We can build a ,"
FISHING POLE

says .
PABLO

"We have a STICK

and a PAPER CLIP for the hook.

All we need is some ."
STRING

"Hey, where did that come from?"

STRING

asks 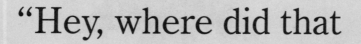.

TYRONE

"Ahoy! We are really not

alone!" says .

UNIQUA

"Follow that  !"
STRING
cries PABLO .
"Ahoy! Who can it be?"

"It is 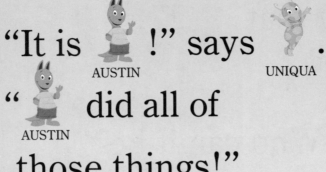 !" says 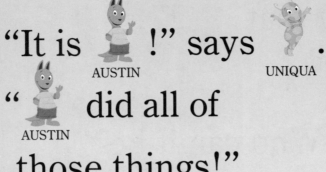 .

AUSTIN

UNIQUA

" did all of

AUSTIN

those things!"

", you should have said 'Ahoy!'"  tells him.

AUSTIN

UNIQUA

53

"I was feeling too shy
to say 'Ahoy!'" says .
AUSTIN
"But I wanted to help."

"That was very nice!"

says  PABLO .

"You are a great castaway."

"Does anyone want a snack?" asks  .

UNIQUA

"Come on! We can have island 🍌 !"

FRUIT

Ahoy!

Riding the Range

adapted by Justin Spelvin
based on the original teleplay by McPaul Smith
illustrated by The Artifact Group

"Yeehaw! I am a cowboy!"

says  TYRONE . "Whose  ROPE is this?"

Cowboy  TYRONE sets out

to find the  ROPE 's owner.

"Hey! My was
ROPE

in the  , but now
SANDBOX

it is gone!" says  .
UNIQUA

"Look!"  says. " ![footprints] !"
PABLO   FOOTPRINTS

"Cowboy ![boots] made these
         BOOTS

![footprints] !" says ![Tasha] .
FOOTPRINTS   TASHA

"There is a bandit on the loose," says  PABLO. "We need to find him!"

PABLO , TASHA , and UNIQUA

put on their HATS and climb

on to their HORSES .

63

"The 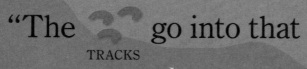 go into that
TRACKS

canyon," says.
PABLO

"It is dark," says .
TASHA

 ,  , and  ride

PABLO   TASHA   UNIQUA

into the canyon.

Soon they are lost!

"How do we get out?"

asks  .

TASHA

"The walls are too tall,"

 says.

UNIQUA

66

Then someone calls out,

"Howdy, down there!"

It is Cowboy !

TYRONE

"When your  sees an ,"

HORSE APPLE

says , "it will climb out.

TYRONE

 love !"  takes

HORSES APPLES TYRONE

an  from his .

APPLE BAG

The  climb toward the 🍎 !

HORSES   APPLE

🐧 , 🦛 , and 🐜 thank

PABLO   TASHA   UNIQUA

🦛 for his help.

TYRONE

69

"We are looking for a bandit,"  says.

PABLO

"But it is too dark to look now," says  .

TYRONE

"It is time to sleep,"
 says.
TASHA

The next day  wakes up

TYRONE

and gets on his .

HORSE

"I will let the others sleep,"

says .

TYRONE

72

As rides away,
TYRONE

 fall from his !
APPLES   BAG

The other 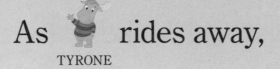 are hungry,
HORSES

so they follow the !
APPLES

73

 ,  , and  wake up.

PABLO   TASHA   UNIQUA

 and the  are gone!

TYRONE   HORSES

"The bandit took them!"

says  .

PABLO

74

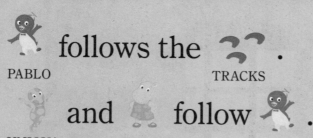

follows the 🐾 **.**

PABLO   TRACKS

 and 🐑 **follow** 🐧 **.**

UNIQUA   TASHA   PABLO

"The bandit must be in

that 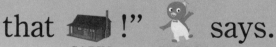!" says.
CABIN   PABLO

 , , and

PABLO   TASHA   UNIQUA

tiptoe to the .
DOOR

Then they rush

into the !
CABIN

77

"Howdy!" says .

TYRONE

 sees 's lasso.

UNIQUA   TYRONE

"That is my !"

JUMP ROPE

"I was looking for the owner,"

says  .

TYRONE

 gives the  back.

TYRONE   JUMP ROPE

Then  tummy rumbles.

UNIQUA'S

"We can go to my  HOUSE

for 🍪 ," 🐧 says.
COOKIES   PABLO

"That is good," says 🫎 .
TYRONE

"I am all out of 🍎 !"
APPLES

80

Rescue Patrol

LEVEL 1

adapted by Catherine Lukas
based on the original teleplay by McPaul Smith
illustrated by The Artifact Group

"We are Mounties on duty!

We have a big job," says .

TYRONE

"We guard a snow ,"

FORT

says .

PABLO

"Inside the  is a big ,"
FORT   SNOWBALL

says .
TYRONE

"Yes," says  PABLO .

"We must guard our SNOWBALL

from SNOWBALL burglars."

85

"We are  patrollers!

SKI

We have a big job!"

says  .

UNIQUA

"Yes," says  .
TASHA

"We rescue people

who are stuck

in the ❄❄ ."
SNOW

"Yum! That hot  COCOA

smells good," says UNIQUA.

"We save the  COCOA

for the people

we rescue!" says TASHA.

" 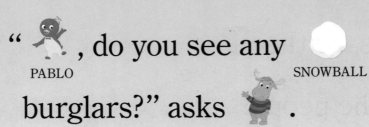, do you see any

PABLO SNOWBALL

burglars?" asks **TYRONE**.

"Not yet," says .

PABLO

"Do you see anyone who needs help in the  ?"

SNOW

asks TASHA.

"Not yet," says .

UNIQUA

"Look! Someone is coming!"

says .

TYRONE

"Help me close the  !"

DOOR

"I heard a call for help!"

says .

TASHA

"It came from that  !"

FORT

"  patrollers to the rescue!"

SKI

says .

UNIQUA

"To the roof!" says  TYRONE .

"We can see better

from up there!"

"We can climb this  ."

LADDER

The  LADDER slips on the ice .

 and

PABLO   TYRONE

land in the soft .

SNOW

99

 and

TASHA   UNIQUA

pull  and

PABLO   TYRONE

out of the  .

SNOW

"We saved you!" says  .

TASHA

100

"Thanks," says .
PABLO

"We must have scared

away the  burglars,"
SNOWBALL

says .
TYRONE

101

"We Mounties did our job!"

says .

TYRONE

"We ⛷ patrollers did our job!"
SKI

says 🦛.
TASHA

"Who wants a snack?"

asks  .

UNIQUA

"We have hot !"

COCOA

Trouble on the Train
on the

by Catherine Lukas
illustrated by The Artifact Group

Cowboy  and Cowgirl

AUSTIN   UNIQUA

take a break from herding cows.

"Here comes a ,"

TRAIN

says Cowgirl .

UNIQUA

"That  is carrying
TRAIN

a  of barbecue sauce,"
BOTTLE

says Cowgirl  .
UNIQUA

"The sauce is on its way to Cooking Cowboy  .

TYRONE

He makes the best

BURGERS in the West!"

Someone else

is watching the  too.
TRAIN

"Ready to rob that ,
TRAIN

Bandit ?"
PABLO

asks Bandit .
TASHA

"Yes I am, Bandit ,"
TASHA

says Bandit .
PABLO

"I hear there is a  BOTTLE

of special sauce on that !"

TRAIN

says Bandit .

PABLO

112

"I will use this  ROPE to try to grab the BOTTLE !" says Bandit TASHA .

113

"If we get that  BOTTLE of sauce,

we can become the best

bandit cooks in the West!"

says Bandit PABLO.

114

Bandit 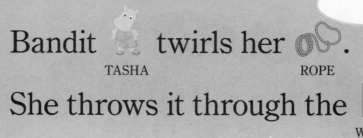 twirls her .
TASHA   ROPE

She throws it through the .
WINDOW

She lassoes the  !

BOTTLE

"Look! Bandits!" says Cowboy  .

AUSTIN

"They just stole the  !"

BOTTLE

118

"After them!"

says Cowgirl UNIQUA.

Cowboy  and Cowgirl

AUSTIN UNIQUA

hop onto their .

HORSES

120

They chase the bandits.

"Watch out!"

yells Bandit  .

TASHA

"  in the road!"

PICKLES

122

It is too late.

Bandit  PABLO and his HORSE

skid and slide on the PICKLES.

123

Bandit drops the 🍾 .

PABLO BOTTLE

Cowgirl catches it.

UNIQUA

"Good work!"

says a voice.

It is Cooking Cowboy  !

TYRONE

"We just wanted to be the best bandit cooks in the West," says Bandit  sadly.

TASHA

"You do not need to be bandits!"

says Cooking Cowboy  TYRONE.

"You can be cowboy cooks

with me instead!"

"Yes, sir," says Cowgirl  .

UNIQUA

"These surely are the best BURGERS

in the West!"

128

A Royal Valentine

by Wendy Wax
illustrated by Susan Hall

Meet Queen !
TASHA

Queen  made a
TASHA   VALENTINE

for her best friend,

Queen .
UNIQUA

 and will bring

TYRONE   PABLO

the to Queen

VALENTINE   UNIQUA

in her 🏰 far away.

PALACE

133

"Nothing can stop us!"

says  .

TYRONE

134

"Not , or  ,
WIND   SNOW

or the  wide!"
RIVER

 says.
PABLO

135

The 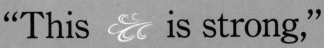 blows.
WIND

"This 🌬 is strong,"
WIND

says .
PABLO

" will not stop us!"

WIND

says  .

TYRONE

137

 starts to fall.
SNOW

"  will not stop us!"
SNOW

says  .
PABLO

"I have .
GOGGLES

Now we can see the ."
PATH

"There is a wide  ,"
RIVER
says  .
PABLO
"How will we cross?"

"I know!"  says.
TYRONE

"We will jump across on

the blocks of ICE ."

"Nothing can stop us!" say  and .

PABLO

TYRONE

"Not , or , or the

WIND

SNOW

 wide!"

RIVER

"Queen , here we come!" shouts .

UNIQUA

TYRONE

At last and
TYRONE   PABLO

reach the .
PALACE

They knock on the .
DOOR

"Who is there?" asks ,
AUSTIN

the guard.
PALACE

"Queen sent us,"
TASHA

say and .
PABLO   TYRONE

"Come in," says .
AUSTIN

"Special  delivery for
VALENTINE

Queen  from Queen ,"
UNIQUA   TASHA

call  and  .
PABLO   TYRONE

"Wow!" says Queen .
UNIQUA

I love it!

I have something

for Queen , too."
TASHA

147

"We will bring it to her,"
 says.

TYRONE

"Nothing can stop us!"

says .

PABLO

"I must give it to

Queen myself,"

TASHA

says Queen 🧒 .

UNIQUA

"I want to go too!" 🦘 says.

AUSTIN

Queen  ,
UNIQUA

 ,  , and
AUSTIN PABLO TYRONE

go to see Queen  .
TASHA

"Special delivery for

Queen ,"
TASHA

says Queen .
UNIQUA

"What is it?" asks

Queen .
TASHA

"It is a big hug.

Happy Valentine's Day!"

Three Wishes

by Catherine Lukas
illustrated by Susan Hall

Castaways  , ,
TYRONE PABLO

and are stuck
TASHA

on an .
ISLAND

155

"I am thirsty,"

says  .

TYRONE

"I am bored,"

says .

PABLO

156

"I am tired
of wearing rags,"
says  .
TASHA

"Look! A !"

BOTTLE

says .

TYRONE

 wades in and gets it.

PABLO

158

dries it off.

TASHA

WHOOSH!

 puffs out

SMOKE

of the ! !

BOTTLE

159

"I am Genie  !
UNIQUA
You may have **3** wishes!"
THREE
"A genie? Cool!"

says  .
TYRONE

161

"I am thirsty,"

says .

TYRONE

"I wish I had a huge,

cold of juice!"

GLASS

"Your wish is my command," says Genie UNIQUA.
WHOOSH!

"I wish I had something

new to do," says .

PABLO

"Your wish is my command,"
says Genie  UNIQUA .
POOF!

"I wish I had something nice to wear," says  .

TASHA

"Your wish is my command,"

says Genie UNIQUA .

ZAP!

"That is  3 wishes,"
THREE

says Genie .
UNIQUA

"My work here is done!"

"But how will we get off this ?" asks .

ISLAND

TASHA

"Wait! I have an idea!"
says .
TYRONE

171

"Maybe we can put our wishes together."

"The  can be a boat.
SURFBOARD
The ⬩ can be a mast,
STRAW
and the ⬩, a sail."
DRESS

"Cool! You made a  !"

SAILBOAT

says Genie .

UNIQUA

"But sailing home will take too long. I am hungry!" ZAP!

"Time for a snack!"

says  .
UNIQUA

"And a cold  of juice!"
GLASS

says  .
TYRONE

Super Spies

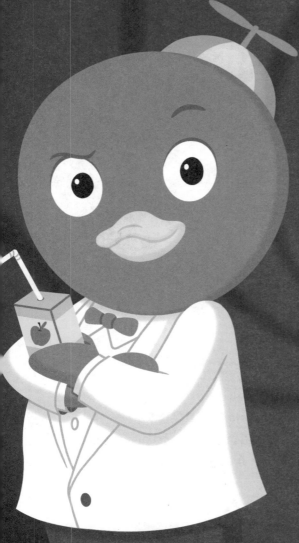

adapted by Alison Inches
based on a teleplay written by Robert Scull
illustrated by A&J Studios

Hello, I am  AGENT SECRET .

I am a Super Spy.

I have to find **3** secret .
THREE   CONTAINERS

1 is in the .
CONTAINER ONE   CITY

2 is in the .
CONTAINER TWO   MOUNTAINS

3 is at the .
CONTAINER THREE   BEACH

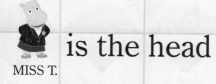 is the head

of the spy agency.

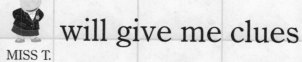 will give me clues

to help me find the .

CONTAINERS

I zoom to the  CITY in my CAR.

I stop at an ICE CREAM shop.

I order a BANANA split.

appears in the  split!

BANANA

She gives me a clue.

Secret CONTAINER ONE 1

is in the Glass BUILDING.

I zip to the Glass  BUILDING .

I grab the CONTAINER .

Uh-oh! The LADY IN PINK !

The LADY IN PINK and HENCHMAN TYRONE

are the bad guys.

No problem!

My is also a .

CAR   HELICOPTER

I get away!

I zoom to the .
MOUNTAINS

I get a .
HOT DOG

The hot dog is really a  .
PHONE

 is on the  .
MISS T.   PHONE

She sends me to the Dairy  .
FARM

187

At the Dairy
FARM

I grab secret 2.
CONTAINER TWO

Uh-oh! The !
LADY IN PINK

No problem!

My 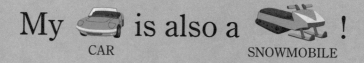 is also a SNOWMOBILE !

CAR   SNOWMOBILE

I get away again.

Now I zoom to the  BEACH .

I walk into a JUICE bar.

I order a SNOW CONE .

MISS T. appears in the SNOW CONE.

She sends me to an ISLAND.

191

At the  ISLAND

I grab secret CONTAINER THREE.

Uh-oh! The LADY IN PINK again!

No problem!

My  is also a !
BOAT   JET

I jet away.

Now I have all **3** !
THREE CONTAINERS

Not so fast!

The  has  !
LADY IN PINK   MISS T.

The  says,
LADY IN PINK

"Hand over the  !"
CONTAINERS

194

She opens the .
CONTAINERS

She finds a ,
GLASS

 , and syrup.
MILK   CHOCOLATE

The secret is   !
CHOCOLATE   MILK

The says
LADY IN PINK

the is hers!
CHOCOLATE   MILK

All hers!

Oops!

The syrup is falling!

CHOCOLATE

The 🧍 is falling too!

LADY IN PINK

197

"I will save you!" I say.

So I save the .

LADY IN PINK

Now the and

want to be good guys!

A toast!

CHOCOLATE   MILK   for everyone!

Hip, hip, hooray!